The Three Silly Girls Grubb

John and Ann Hassett

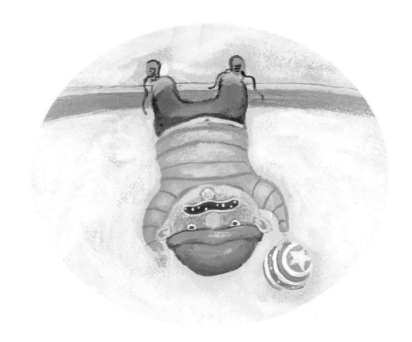

Houghton Mifflin Company Boston

Walter Lorraine Books

For Katrinka and Bitz

Walter Lorraine (wr) Books

www.houghtonmifflinbooks.com

Library of Congress Cataloging-in-Publication Data
Hassett, John.
    The three silly girls Grubb / John and Ann Hassett.
        p. cm.
    Summary: In this revision of the familiar tale "The Three Billy Goats Gruff," three
sisters manage to outwit Ugly-Boy Bobby who spends his time under the bridge they
must cross on their way to school.
    RNF ISBN 0-618-14183-9   PA ISBN 0-618-69334-3
    [1. Fairy tales. 2. Folklore.] I. Hassett, Ann.
PZ8.H263 Th 2002
[398.2]—dc21
[E]
                                        2001039535

ISBN-13: 978-0-618-69334-4

Printed in Singapore
TWP 15 14 13 12 11 10 9 8 7 6 5

The Three Silly Girls Grubb

Once there were three silly sisters named Grubb.
They came in three sizes — small, medium, and extra large.
One morning the three silly sisters missed the bus,
so they had to cross a bridge to get to school.

In a hole under the bridge hid Ugly-Boy
Bobby. Ugly-Boy Bobby never went to school.
He was the kind of boy who ate bugs,
tossed stones at cats, and
drank from puddles —
the muddier the better.

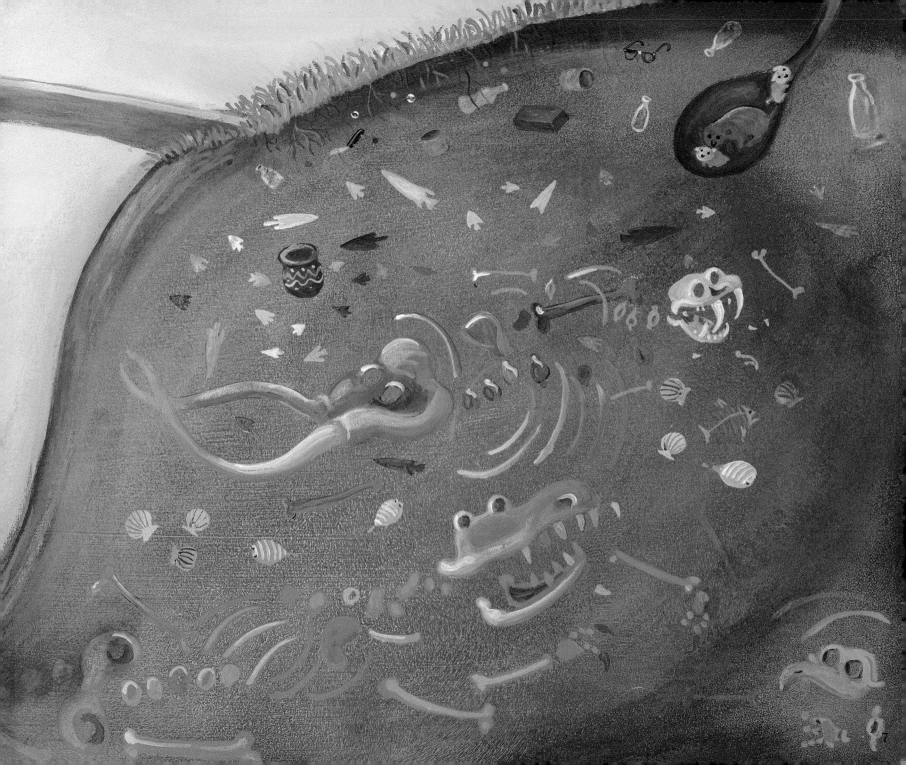

The smallest of the Grubbs skipped over the
bridge on her way to school, skippity-skip-skip.
"Who's that skipping on my bridge?"
grunted a voice from the hole.

"It is little me,"
squeaked the smallest of the three.
"I am on my way to school to
count to ten on my toes."

"Not before I eat your lunch,"
grumbled Ugly-Boy Bobby.
"Oh please do not,"
said the smallest girl.
"I have only one jelly-donut.
Wait for my sister,
the medium-sized Grubb.
She brings six jelly-donuts
for her lunch."

"Go, or I will stuff toads in your sneakers,"
grunted Ugly-Boy Bobby.
The first sister ran to school
as fast as her little-sized legs could go.

Soon the second sister
skipped over the bridge
on her way to school,
skippity-skip-skip.

"Who's that skipping on my bridge?"
grunted the voice from the hole.

"It is middle-sized me,"
said the second of the three.
"I am on my way to school
to spell *bumblebee's bum*."

"Not before I eat your lunch,"
growled Ugly-Boy Bobby, gnashing his teeth.
"Oh please do not," said the second girl.
"I have only six jelly-donuts. Wait for my sister,
the biggest Grubb. She brings a dozen
jelly-donuts for her lunch."

18

"Go, or I will tangle bats in your hair,"
grunted Ugly-Boy Bobby.
The second sister ran to school
as fast as her medium-sized legs could go.

The biggest of the Grubbs skipped over the bridge,
skippity-skip-skip.

"Who's that skipping on my bridge?"
grunted the voice.

"It is big-sized me," said the biggest of the three.
"I am on my way to school to see itsy-bitsy, teeny-tiny
things under a microscope."
"Not before I eat your dozen jelly-donuts,"
roared Ugly-Boy Bobby smacking his ugly-boy lips.

He hauled himself
up onto the bridge.
He stomped
his ugly-boy feet.
He shook
his ugly-boy fists.

The extra-large girl only grinned.
"You may have my dozen jelly-donuts,"
she said. "But first I will plant a dozen
mushy kisses on your little-boy nose."
The biggest girl puckered up
her extra-large-sized lips.

Ugly-Boy Bobby leaped from the bridge.
He ran off to school as fast-fast-fast as
his ugly-boy legs could go,
and he never missed school again.

Nowadays, Ugly-Boy Bobby is called just Robert.
He can count to ten on his fingers.
He can spell *bumblebee's bum*.
He can see small things under a microscope,
if he wears his glasses.

Spink! Spank! Spinach!
This story is finished.